TWO SMART COOKIES

BOOK SERIES

Published By

OHC Group LLC
PO Box 7839, Westlake Village, CA 91359

SECOND EDITION
ISBN 0-9763213-5-1

Printed and bound in China

The Only Hearts Girls™ formed
The Only Hearts Club® in a bond
of true friendship. They are a fun-
loving bunch of friends who are
always there for one another. They
laugh, share secrets and have the
greatest adventures together. Most
importantly, they encourage one
another to think with their hearts
and to try and do the right thing.

Contents

Anna Gets Cookin'

Anna Sophia was sitting at the kitchen table, browsing through a stack of cookbooks. She loved to cook and bake, especially with her friends from the Only Hearts Club, a fun-loving group of six girls who were always there for one another. They laughed, shared secrets and had the greatest adventures together. Most importantly, they thought with their hearts and tried to do the right thing, even though it wasn't always easy.

Anna particularly enjoyed cooking or baking when there was a special occasion. This month, two special things were happening! Saint Francis Hospital was having its annual carnival, which included a "Best Dessert" bake-off competition. The winner would get a blue ribbon and a professional chef's hat, and have his or her recipe included in a celebrity cookbook. Anna got the second piece of good news from her mother.

"Guess who's coming for a visit!" her mother said, walking into the kitchen. Anna guessed wrong three times. "No, no and no," her mother said. "Nana's coming!"

"Hurray!" Anna cried. She loved it when her grandmother came to visit from Mexico. She always spent lots of time with Anna, sharing funny family stories and teaching her delicious new recipes. Nana's cooking was all the more amazing because she not only created her own recipes, but she often didn't even have to measure ingredients as she cooked. She just somehow seemed to know how much of each ingredient to use, and the food always turned out delicious! It was fun for Anna to cook with her Nana because they always ended up covered in flour, singing, laughing and sampling their tasty treats.

"Nana's never been to the carnival before. We can go together, but don't tell her we're entering the bake-off," Anna said as she scanned her favorite cookbooks for a special treat to make for the competition. "I want to surprise her." Anna stopped on a page with a picture of a scrumptious-looking chocolate dessert. "Yum!" she cried. "This chocolate pecan pie looks delicious!"

She immediately began pulling pie pans and mixing bowls from the cupboards.

"You'd better check to make sure we have all the ingredients first," her mother said with a chuckle.

"Thanks, Mom," Anna replied. "I guess I get a little ahead of myself. Oh! And I have to talk it over with Olivia first. We're entering the contest together."

"That'll be fun," Anna's mother said. "And that's very considerate of you to check with Olivia first. You want to find a recipe that you'll both like to make and eat."

"Well, it's only fair. And I know she'd do it for me," Anna said as she picked up the phone. "I'll give her a call now."

Anna scanned the refrigerator and cupboards. They were stocked with all sorts of delicious foods because her grandmother was coming. As she spoke with Olivia on the phone, Anna knew she had all the ingredients they needed to make the chocolate pecan pie she had seen in her cookbook. She described it to Olivia.

"Yummmmmy! It sounds great!" Olivia said.

"Can you come over and help me bake one of these

pies so we can practice for the contest?" asked Anna.
Olivia said she'd be right over.

Shaking and Baking

A little while later Olivia arrived at Anna's house. As she eyed the chocolate chips, pecans, and shredded coconut on the counter, Olivia's stomach started making funny sounds. "Just thinking about it makes me hungry," she smiled as she patted her tummy. Even her yellow Labrador retriever, Sniff, wanted a taste. He sat up, raised his front paws and stuck out his tongue.

"No, silly," Olivia laughed to Sniff. "This is people food, not dog food!"

"Here," said Anna, handing Olivia some dogs treats. Turning to her cocker spaniel, Bubulina, she said, "Want to go outside and play with Sniff?" Bubulina barked as if she understood. The girls let the dogs out onto the back deck, where they shared the treats, played with their toys, and then cuddled together in the shade in Bubulina's dog bed.

"How cute are they?" Olivia smiled.

"Best dogs ever!" Anna replied. "OK, now that they're settled, let's get back to baking!"

Anna had removed the frozen pie shell from the freezer, and it was just about thawed out. "First, we have to bake the pie shell for ten minutes at 350 degrees," she said.

Anna's mother set the oven and Olivia slid the pie shell onto the rack and closed the oven door. "You chop the pecans and keep an eye on the pie shell," Anna said. "I'll measure the sugar and the butter."

"How about some music?" Olivia asked, turning on the CD player. She put on one of their favorite CDs. "Oh, I love this one!" she said as she sang along with it and began to dance around.

Anna turned her attention to measuring the sugar and butter. She couldn't help dancing to the music, too. Olivia tapped her feet as she chopped a pile of pecans. The two friends sang along louder and louder with the music. Although they were wrapped up in the song, they didn't miss a beat when it came to

measuring, mixing and checking the pie. Before long, it was already time for Anna's mother to remove the finished pie from the oven.

"Wow!" said Anna. "It looks delicious! I'll bet we'll win with this recipe for sure."

Olivia agreed. "Everyone loves chocolate...and pies. We'll definitely win!"

Practice Makes Perfect

Olivia and Anna were excited about the bake-off, and they filled out the entry form very carefully. A few days later Anna received a notice in the mail.

"Olivia," she said when her friend answered the phone, "We're in. We've been assigned to table number 12 for the competition." Anna could hear Olivia's dog barking in the background. "I guess Sniff's excited, too!" she said. They both laughed.

"Almost as much as I am," said Olivia. "Looks like there's nothing to do but wait for the bake-off and get our blue ribbon! When is your Nana coming?"

"Saturday, the same day as the carnival," Anna replied. "I can hardly wait to see her! I want to surprise her with our entry in the contest. She'll be so proud!"

"That'll be great," Olivia said, then paused. "Do you think we should practice the chocolate pecan pie one more time before the cook-off?"

"I guess it wouldn't hurt," Anna said.

Later that day, Olivia met Anna at her house, and they baked another chocolate pecan pie. They followed the same sequence of steps: measuring, mixing, chopping, baking – and of course, tasting. The pie looked, smelled and tasted the same. The girls were now even more confident that they would win.

"It'll be fun to show my Nana our blue ribbon," Anna said.

Saturday morning had come so fast. Shortly after Anna got dressed, there was a knock at her front door.

"Hi, Olivia," she said, holding the door open for her friend and her dog, Sniff.

"I'm so excited about the bake-off today!" Olivia said, taking out fresh ingredients from paper bags and spreading them across Anna's kitchen table.

"So, what should we do when we become famous because of our great chocolate pecan pie?" Olivia asked casually as they greased the pie pan.

"I don't know," said Anna. "Maybe we'll get our own TV show where we can make fun recipes every day! We'll call it *The Only Hearts Chefs Show!* They both giggled.

Just then, Anna's mother came into the kitchen. "Are you girls ready to make your prize-winning pie now?" she asked with a smile.

The girls nodded and clapped. "Yes! Yes!" they said excitedly.

"All right, I'll preheat the oven for you," her mother said. "Make sure you set your timer so I know when to take the pie out. We'll have just enough time to bake the pie and let it cool before heading over to the carnival for the bake-off!"

"OK, Mom," Anna said.

Then, as rehearsed, the girls gathered their ingredients and quickly chopped and mixed them. Before long, the pie was in the oven and the kitchen was filled with the familiar, delicious smell of chocolate and pecans. Soon the oven timer sounded, and Anna's mother helped the girls take the hot pie out of the oven.

"Let's set it on the picnic table outside to cool for a minute," suggested Anna.

"OK, but be careful carrying it!" said Olivia. "If we drop it, we don't have ingredients to make another one!"

Anna put on her favorite yellow-and-red oven mittens and picked up the pie. She walked slowly and carefully, taking little baby steps toward the door. Both she and Olivia let out big sighs of relief when Anna finally placed the pie on the picnic table.

When they got back inside, Olivia put on their favorite CD again. After all, this was as good a time as any for a well-deserved pre-celebration! When their favorite song came on, Olivia turned up the music almost as loud as it would go and the two girls sang along to it. Olivia took one of the mixers in her hand and Anna grabbed a spatula. They held them up to their mouths, pretending they were microphones. They danced this way and that, moving from the window, where they sang to their dogs outside, to the living room and then back to the kitchen.

Just as the song ended, Bubulina and Sniff came bounding into the kitchen, their tails wagging. Olivia noticed that Sniff's face looked like it was covered with mud…and so was Bubulina's! "Hey, have you guys been digging in the garden again?" she asked the dogs. "Look at our puppies, Anna, they're all muddy!" she smiled.

"Well *this* mud sure smells good…" Anna laughed as Bubulina came over to her.

"Yummy mud? Well that's probably why Sniff and Bubulina ate it up!" laughed Olivia.

Anna bent down for a closer look at Bubulina's face. "Oh, *NO!*" she cried suddenly.

"What is it?" Olivia asked, startled.

"That's not mud on their faces!" Anna moaned. "It's chocolate!"

"Our pie!" Olivia screamed as the girls ran toward the door.

Sure enough, outside they found a nearly empty pie dish on the floor next to the picnic table, surrounded by lots of chocolate paw prints.

"Oh no," Anna cried again. "We can't enter the bake-off. There's no time to go buy new ingredients and bake another pie before the competition."

The girls looked sadly at the two dogs, which looked back at them with their chocolate-covered faces, tails still wagging.

"Who knew dogs liked chocolate pecan pie?" mumbled Olivia to no one in particular.

Anna Cooks Up a Plan

As Anna and Olivia stared at the empty pie dish, they heard a commotion at the front door. Nana had arrived from the airport! Anna smiled briefly, but then remembered what had just happened. Her smile turned to a frown. Now she wouldn't be able to enter the bake-off and surprise her Nana. Anna walked slowly toward the front door to welcome her grandmother.

"Well hello, beautiful!" exclaimed Nana as soon as she saw Anna. "And hello Olivia!" Anna smiled weakly as she hugged Nana.

Nana could tell something was not right. She looked at Anna's face. "What's wrong with my little princess?" she asked.

Anna was about to tell her what had happened when she suddenly had an idea! "Um, Nana?" she started. "I missed you so much and can't wait to start cooking with you!"

Olivia gave Anna a funny look.

"Oh, well, that's very nice, my dear," said Nana. "Maybe we can cook something for the family tonight for dinner!"

"Uh, well, I was hoping we could cook something like, right now," said Anna.

"Anna!" her mother interrupted. "Nana just walked in the door, for goodness sakes. Let's give her some time to relax and get comfortable."

But Nana could see that Anna was serious about cooking *now*, and she always wanted to make her granddaughter happy. "Oh, I'm perfectly fine," Nana smiled to her daughter. "C'mon Anna, let's do some cooking!"

Anna's mother shook her head and shrugged her shoulders. "Well, OK. I guess I'll go unpack your things and get you settled," she said to Nana. "You are a very lucky granddaughter," she reminded Anna with a smile before she went upstairs.

Anna nodded in agreement.

"What are you up to?" Olivia whispered to Anna as they followed Nana to the kitchen.

"Shhhhh," Anna whispered back. "I think I've figured out how we can still enter that bake-off later today."

Jumble Cookies!

W ell, what are we cooking?" Nana asked, washing her hands in the kitchen sink and putting on the apron she had found in the pantry.

"Uh, I was thinking of baking rather than cooking," said Anna.

Nana raised her eyebrows. "OK, baking it is. Now what are we baking?"

"Well, um, we didn't really have a specific recipe in mind…" started Anna.

Nana thought for a moment. "So what ingredients do we have?"

Anna opened the cupboards and the refrigerator. "Oh, we have just about everything," Anna said.

Except for making chocolate pecan pie, Olivia thought to herself.

"Well why don't we take our time and bake a pot pie that we can all share for dinner?" asked Nana.

"No, I was thinking more like a dessert," said Anna. "And something we could whip up really fast! Hey, I remember one time you made cookies out of a whole bunch of ingredients in just few minutes. What were those called again?"

"You mean my jumble cookies?" asked Nana.

Anna thought back to a time when she and her grandmother had spent the day baking pies together. When they had finished, they had a few leftover apples, some cherries, a half-cup of coconut, cinnamon, and a handful of pecans. Instead of throwing the leftovers out, Nana added them to some other creative ingredients, like peanut butter and marshmallows, and made something she called jumble cookies – cookies filled with a jumble of ingredients.

"Yes! That's it, Nana! Jumble cookies!" said Anna, smiling brightly for the first time since Nana had arrived.

"OK, let's do it!" said Nana, starting to look for ingredients. "And what are we going to do with what will surely be delicious cookies?" she asked.

"Oh, I don't know, maybe share them with friends," fibbed Anna, brushing off the question. But inside, she knew exactly what she was planning to do with those cookies. She was going to enter them in the bake-off at the carnival! Olivia thought she knew what Anna was up to, and she gave Anna a funny look. Thinking about what she planned to do with those cookies gave Anna an uncomfortable feeling in her heart, but she ignored it.

Nana Makes It Happen

Before Anna and Olivia knew it, Nana was flying around the kitchen, opening up the cupboards and lining up all the goodies she could find – chocolate chips, marshmallows, raisins, oatmeal, dried apricots, cinnamon, granola, vanilla and the leftover coconuts and pecans from the ingredients for the chocolate pecan pie. She even found a handful of jellybeans for color.

A little while later, just as Nana was getting ready to put the cookie dough on the baking sheet, she suddenly stopped and realized that other than handing her a few ingredients and cooking utensils, Anna and Olivia had just been standing there watching her do all the work!

"Whoops!" Nana exclaimed with a smile. "I get so excited about cooking, I almost forgot to ask you girls to help me! I'm almost done, but you still can help.

27

You can do what I'm doing. Take a teaspoon of the cookie dough and drop it onto the baking sheet. Can you do that?"

Anna and Olivia looked at each other and smiled. They knew that also meant you got to lick the cooking bowl and the spoons! "Sure, Nana!" they said in unison. These *were* going to be delicious cookies!

As soon as the cookies were out of the oven, Anna rushed to put them into a basket with a handle. She knew she was running out of time to get to the carnival for the competition.

"Anna, Anna! Slow down!" warned Nana gently. "Those cookies are still very hot!"

"Yeah, what's the big rush?" asked Olivia suspiciously as she narrowed her eyes.

Anna gave Olivia a look. "Remember, Olivia," she started. "We have to go see our, um, *friends* right now, and we promised we'd *bake* something for the um, *party?*"

Olivia shook her head but Nana didn't see it. Her suspicion was correct! Anna was planning to enter these cookies in the carnival bake-off!

Within minutes, Anna had the cookies in the basket covered with tin foil, and she and Olivia were running out the front door to get on their bikes and race off to the carnival. Anna hung the basket from her handlebars.

"Have fun with your friends!" called Nana from the front door. "I hope they like the cookies!"

Anna realized that in her hurry, she'd forgotten to thank Nana! She ran toward the house and gave Nana a big hug. "Thanks, Nana!" she grinned.

"Oh, Anna, thank *you*," said Nana, hugging her close. "Thank you for spending time with me and doing nice things for other people. You are such a good girl!"

Though Nana's words were nice, they certainly didn't make Anna feel very good. In fact, they made that odd feeling in her heart get even stronger. But Anna didn't have time to think about that right now. She *had* to get the carnival with the cookies before it was too late!

In a matter of seconds, she was back on her bike and she and Olivia were pedaling furiously to the carnival.

"I hope you know what you're doing," said Olivia as she rode next to Anna.

Anna didn't respond. She just stared forward and made sure to balance the basket of jumble cookies as they rode over the hill and the top of the Ferris wheel from the carnival appeared.

The Bake-Off

Sure enough, a large crowd was gathering at the competition, eager to see who would get the award for having baked the best dessert. As they arrived, the girls saw that their table number 12 was empty, and the judges were huddled together at the judges' table up on the stage. Were they too late?

The woman at the table next to them, who had a delicious-looking lemon pie in front of her, saw their worried looks and said, "I think the judges are almost ready to make their decision. You better let them know you're here."

Anna and Olivia ran to the stage to explain that they had just arrived and to see if they still had time to enter the competition.

"Well, you are sort of late," said a judge who had big strawberry blond curls and large blue-tinted glasses. She made a mark on her clipboard. Olivia and Anna swallowed hard.

"Yes, ma'am," Anna started. "We, um, had an accident with our pie. So we rushed to bake these cookies instead." As soon as the words came out of her mouth, Anna had that funny feeling in heart again.

"Let me discuss this matter with the other judges," said the judge.

The five judges huddled to talk it over.

"What do you mean 'we' baked these cookies?" Olivia whispered to Anna with a quizzical look.

"Well, we did...sort of," Anna whispered back. "I mean, we helped, right?" Anna sounded like she was trying to convince herself more than she was trying to convince Olivia.

"Annnnnnaaaa," Olivia whispered. "We barely did anything! I don't think licking the spoons counts as baking!"

"Shhhhh…" said Anna.

Just then the judge turned around to face them. "OK," she said. "We'll let you young ladies be a part of the bake-off. Let's see what you've got!"

Anna and Olivia just nodded quietly.

"These are our very own creation," said Anna. "We call them jumble cookies. Please have as many as you like."

Each judge tried a cookie, smiled and nodded, and then made some notes on his or her notepad. Soon they were back at the judges' table on the stage, looking over their notes and discussing who would win the award.

Anna Listens to Her Heart

After what seemed like a long time, one of the judges stepped to the microphone on the stage and said, "Everyone, may I have your attention please?"

The crowd got quiet. Anna and Olivia stood behind table number 12, up front with the other competitors.

"We are pleased to announce the winner, actually the *two* winners, in the annual carnival bake-off!" said the judge with a big smile.

The crowd buzzed with excitement.

"The winners are Anna Sophia and Olivia Hope, at table number 12 with their cookie creation!"

There was a great deal of applause. Anna looked out into the crowd and saw her friends from The Only Hearts Club, Taylor Angelique, Karina Grace, Briana Joy and Lily Rose. They had all just arrived at the bake-off and were cheering for Anna and Olivia. Now

Anna had that feeling in her heart again. What had she done? They had won first prize for cookies they hadn't even baked themselves! She knew that she could no longer ignore the feeling in her heart.

"Will our baking champions please come up on the stage to receive their award?!" boomed the judge over the microphone.

Anna and Olivia climbed the steps to the stage slowly, and went to stand next to the judge at the microphone.

"Everyone, I'm pleased to introduce Anna Sophia and Olivia Hope!" the judge announced. "They are our winners for having baked the most delicious cookies! Girls, please tell the folks how you came up with this wonderful dessert!"

The judge handed the microphone to Anna. "Thank you for choosing our cookies," she said to the judges. "But I have something I need to tell everyone."

The judge looked at her, as did the silent crowd.

"It's not our recipe, and we didn't bake those cookies," Anna admitted.

There was a gasp from the crowd.

"We had made a chocolate pecan pie to enter in the bake-off this morning, but our dogs decided *they* wanted it for dessert. So we had no dessert to enter in the competition. Then my Nana, I mean, my grandmother, arrived from Mexico to visit my family today, and I asked her to bake these delicious cookies," Anna continued.

Anna looked out at the crowd. Now everyone seemed to be talking and gesturing. The judges had gathered in a tight circle behind their table and were talking among themselves. She put down the microphone.

"Well, I didn't want to admit it, but inside I knew it was wrong to take credit for cookies we didn't bake," Anna said to Olivia. "Now we'll be disqualified and everyone will think we're cheaters."

"But at least you did the right thing and told the truth," Olivia offered.

"My parents are going to be so upset when they find out," said Anna. "And worst of all, my Nana will be so disappointed in me. She's always telling me what a good girl I am, and now she'll think it's not true." Anna looked as though she was about to cry.

And the Winner is...

Suddenly the judge was in front of the microphone again. "Everyone, everyone, can I please have your attention?" the judge asked. "The judges have discussed this matter, and while we appreciate Anna Sophia admitting the truth, we have no choice but to disqualify her and her friend from the bake-off. The winner of this competition is the person who makes the best dessert, and these girls did not bake these cookies."

"I knew it," cried Anna. "This is so embarrassing. Let's just go home."

Just then some familiar voices from the audience caught Anna's attention. "Anna! Anna! Over here!"

Those were her mother and Nana's voices! They had come to the carnival after all! Anna looked out and saw them moving forward through the crowd toward the stage. She ran down the stairs to meet them.

"When did you get here?" she asked

"Oh, right after you and Olivia did," said her mother. She had seen the whole thing and didn't look very pleased.

"I'm so sorry…" Anna started. "I just wanted to…." But the judge was back on the microphone and his voice drowned hers out.

"The judges still feel that the best dessert is the jumble cookies. Therefore, the winner of the Saint Francis Hospital Carnival Bake-Off is…Nana!"

"Huh?" asked Anna, as she spun around to look at the judge. "Nana?"

"Well, of course," said the judge, looking down from the stage with a smile. "She *did* bake these delicious cookies, didn't she?"

Anna wiped away the tears in her eyes. It was true, she realized. The person who made the best dessert was the winner. The judges thought the jumble cookies were the best dessert, and Nana had made the jumble cookies!

"Now I'm just guessing," continued the judge. "But might that lady standing next to you down there be your grandmother?"

Nana didn't say anything, so Anna spoke up in a loud voice. "Yes, this is my grandmother, and I call her Nana."

"Well then," said the judge. "Will the winner of this year's bake-off please come up on the stage and accept her award?"

Nana wasn't used to this sort of attention and shook her head. "Oh, I love to cook and bake," she told Anna, "but I didn't realize I could win a prize for doing it!"

As the crowd cheered for her to go on stage, Nana thought for a moment. Then she had an idea. She held Anna and Olivia's hands and marched up the stairs with them onto the stage.

"Would you like to say a few words?" asked the judge.

Nana nodded and took the microphone. "Thank you," she said to the judges. "I love cooking and baking, and I've been doing it for a long time, but until today, I never, in my entire life, won an award for cooking. It's such a nice feeling!"

Anna smiled and saw that her mother was doing

the same. Everyone in her family knew Nana was a great cook. It made her feel good inside to see her grandmother getting some well-deserved recognition. And Nana looked so proud!

"I have one important thing to say," Nana continued into the microphone. "I have always thought that my granddaughter Anna Sophia is such a fine young lady. And though she didn't know it, I stood in the back of the audience during this competition and watched the whole thing."

Anna started feeling embarrassed again. She was right, she thought. Nana *was* disappointed in her.

Nana continued. "And although she made some mistakes and she may not be perfect, I want everyone to know how proud I am of Anna for listening to her heart today. What she did here wasn't the easy thing to do. She could have just kept quiet about it and nobody would have known the truth, but she chose to do the right thing. I'm so lucky and happy. My granddaughter is indeed a special young lady, and I love her more than ever!"

Anna hugged Nana tight as the crowd applauded. Anna looked down from the stage and saw Taylor, Karina, Briana and Lily smiling at her. Karina gave Anna a "thumbs up" sign. It felt good to do the right thing!

~ Two Smart Cookies ~

Read all the Only Hearts Girls' heartwarming storybooks.

*It's Hard To Say
Good-Bye*
When her friend loses her
dog, Taylor Angelique
finds a new puppy for
her. But will Taylor
Angelique keep the cute
little puppy for herself?

Horse Sense
Olivia Hope's horse
develops a slight limp
right before the big show.
Will she go for the blue
ribbon or choose to save
her horse?

Dancing Dilemma
Karina Grace is the best
dancer in school. Will she
let her talent get in the
way of her friendships?

Teamwork Works
Briana Joy is a superstar
on the soccer field. Will
she try to win the game
by herself or be a good
teammate and help a
friend?

Two Smart Cookies
Anna Sophia's pie is
ruined just hours before
the big bake-off. Can she
whip up Grandma's
secret recipe in time?

Peep for Keeps
Lily Rose discovers a lost
baby bird in the forest.
Should she keep it as a
pet or return it to nature?